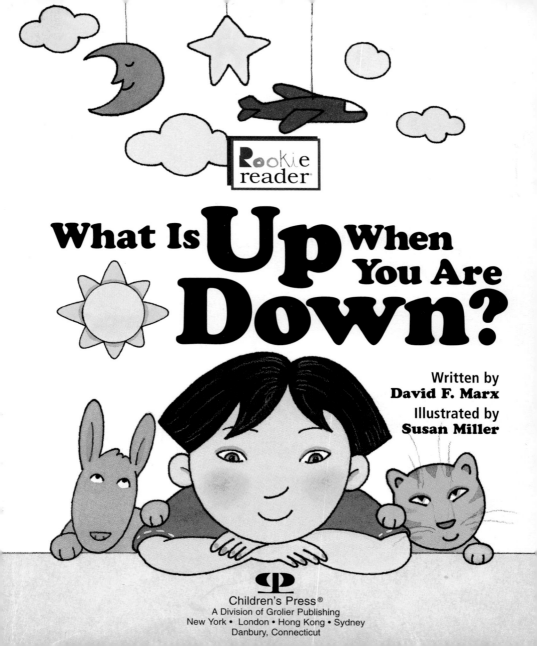

Rookie reader®

What Is Up When You Are Down?

Written by
David F. Marx

Illustrated by
Susan Miller

Children's Press®
A Division of Grolier Publishing
New York • London • Hong Kong • Sydney
Danbury, Connecticut

For Eva, who is always up.
—D.F.M.

For my niece and nephew, Billy and Rachel.
—S.M.

Reading Consultants
Linda Cornwell
Coordinator of School Quality and Professional Improvement
(Indiana State Teachers Association)

Katharine A. Kane
Education Consultant
(Retired, San Diego County Office of Education
and San Diego State University)

Visit Children's Press® on the Internet at:
http://publishing.grolier.com

Library of Congress Cataloging-in-Publication Data
Marx, David F.
    What is up when you are down? / by David F. Marx; illustrated by Susan Miller.
    p. cm. — (Rookie reader)
    Summary: An illustrated series of questions and answers about up and down, in and out, cool and hot.
    ISBN 0-516-22007-1 (lib. bdg.)   0-516-27044-3 (pbk.)
    [1. English Language–Synonyms and antonyms Fiction. 2. Questions and answers.] I. Miller, Susan, ill. II. Title. III. Series.
PZ7.M36822Wh 2000
[E]—dc21   99-15864
                                 CIP

GROLIER
PUBLISHING   1 2 3 4 5 6 7 8 9 10 R 09 08 07 06 05 04 03 02 01 00

What is up when you are down?

Airplanes.
Trees.
The moon.

What is down when you are up?

Cars.
Houses.
Your cat.

9

What is out when you are in?

An airplane.
Trees.
The sun.

13

What is in when you are out?

15

Mom and Dad.
Big sister.
Her dog.

What is cool when you are hot?

19

Juice.
Ice.
Shade.

What is up when you are down?

23

Word List (32 words)

airplane	down	shade
airplanes	her	sister
an	hot	sun
and	houses	the
are	ice	trees
big	in	up
cars	is	what
cat	juice	when
cool	Mom	you
Dad	moon	your
dog	out	

About the Author

David F. Marx is a children's author and editor who lives in Newtown, Connecticut.

About the Illustrator

Susan Miller has been a freelance children's illustrator for more than ten years and has illustrated numerous books and materials for children. She works in her home studio in the rural Litchfield Hills of Connecticut, where she lives with her husband and two school-age children. They provide her endless opportunities for inspiration.